For
Debbie Moody

First published 1994 by Walker Books Ltd
87 Vauxhall Walk, London SE11 5HJ

This edition published 2007

2 4 6 8 10 9 7 5 3

This book has been typeset in AT Arta.

Printed in China

British Library Cataloguing in Publication Data:
a catalogue record for this book is
available from the British Library.

ISBN 978-1-4063-0988-1

www.walkerbooks.co.uk

Mrs Pirate

Nick Sharratt

WALKER BOOKS

AND SUBSIDIARIES

LONDON · BOSTON · SYDNEY · AUCKLAND

When Mrs Pirate
went shopping,
she bought
an apple pie

and a patch
for her eye,

a bar
of soap

and a
telescope,

an onion
and a carrot

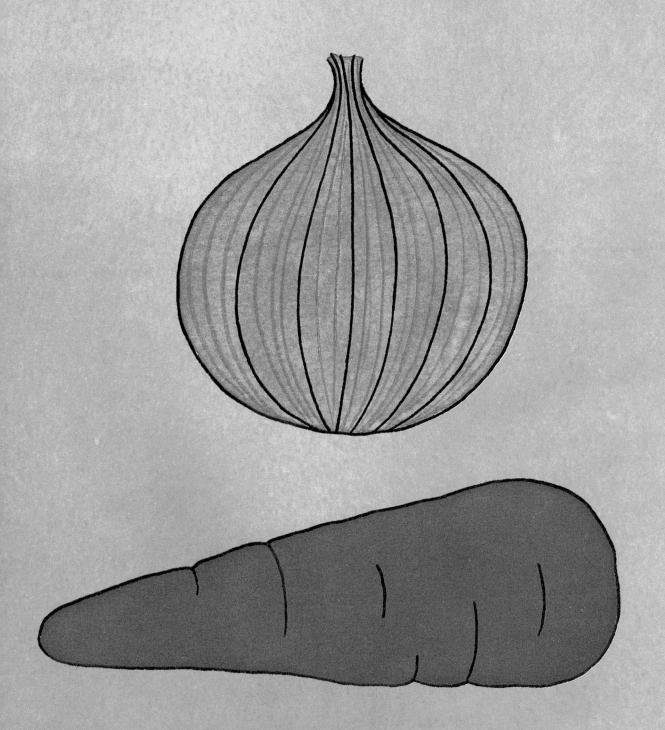

and a red and
green parrot,

some knickers
and a vest

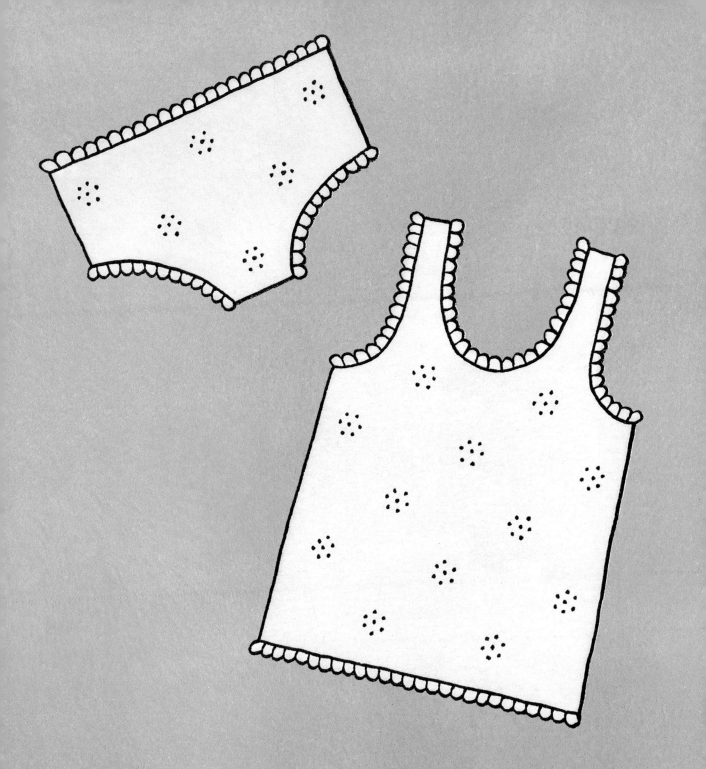

and an old
treasure chest,

buttons for
her coat

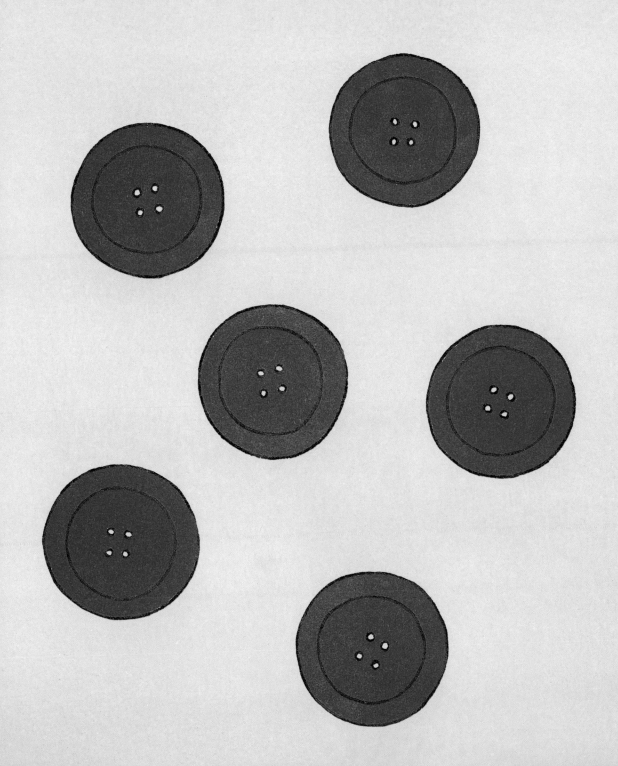

and a big
sailing boat,

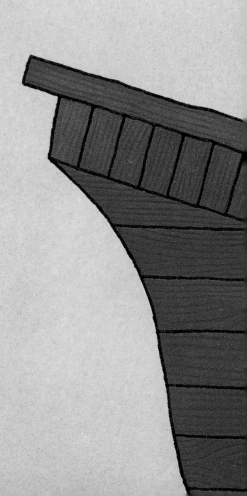

a packet
of tea

and some
sea.